For my dad, who howled at the moon,
and for everyone who called him Tapa
S. S.

For my dear dad, whom I loved so much.
You are the star I will look for in the universe.
C. D.

First edition 2020

Library of Congress Catalog Card Number pending
ISBN 978-0-7636-9834-8

19 20 21 22 23 24 CCP 10 9 8 7 6 5 4 3 2 1

Printed in Shenzhen, Guangdong, China

This book was typeset in Playfair.
The illustrations were done in ink.

Candlewick Press
99 Dover Street
Somerville, Massachusetts 02144

visit us at www.candlewick.com

The Stars
Just Up the Street

Sue Soltis   illustrated by Christine Davenier

CANDLEWICK PRESS

Mabel loved the stars.

She could count five from her window when it wasn't cloudy,
and nineteen from her backyard in a narrow patch of sky.

Her grandfather loved to tell stories, and Mabel listened hardest to the parts about the night sky on the prairie where he grew up.

Once, meteors fell there like rain. Sometimes the full moon rose so big, he said, it looked like another planet.

And every night, there were thousands of stars.

Thousands? Mabel knew something was wrong.

She climbed the tallest tree out back.

"Even from up here," she called down to Grandpa, "I only count thirty-seven."

"Well," Grandpa said, "I think we can see more stars on the hill just up the street. The sky is wide there, and I bet it's darker."

They took a walk.

The road wound up and up.

At the top, Mabel started to count.

"Only one hundred and three," she said at last.

Then she noticed all the lit-up windows and porches.

"Maybe people could turn off their lights," she said.

"Maybe they would," Grandpa said.

"Let's ask them," Mabel said, and she took Grandpa's hand.

They went door-to-door. It was a bit hard to explain . . .
and a few people refused.

"I might bump
into the wall."

"I don't want to step
on my cat."

"I'd like to help, but how can I make dinner in the dark?"

"Come outside with us," Mabel suggested. "Just for a bit."

In the end, many of them did just that.

"It's been a long time since I went stargazing," someone said.

"Look, the Big Dipper!" someone else shouted.

"You *can* see more stars!" Mabel said, and she began to count.

At 214 she suddenly stopped. The glow from a nearby streetlight blocked part of the sky.

"Grandpa, who can switch that off?" she asked.

"Well, the town controls the streetlights," Grandpa said.

The next day, Grandpa and Mabel visited the mayor at town hall.

The mayor told them no.

"We keep safe, well-lit streets in this town!" she said.

"Argh," said Mabel as they left town hall. "I guess I can look
at the stars from the tree. Maybe thirty-seven is not so bad."

But on the way home, they ran into the mail carrier
and told him about their meeting with the mayor.

"Hmm," he said, "maybe I'll have a word with the mayor, too."

Then Mabel decided to tell everyone they saw.

They talked to a lady
walking her dog,

a family on their way
to the library,

and a crowd of speedy bicycle riders stopped at a traffic light.

Mabel got really good at getting to the point.

"You won't believe how many more stars we would see," she said.

All through that day, the mayor received phone calls, emails, and even a few in-person visits! But her answer was always no.

"What about burglars?" she said.

"Dark streets don't increase crime," said a police officer.

"What about people falling on dark paths?" the mayor went on.

"Hand out flashlights," suggested a parks and recreation officer.

"There are town regulations!" the mayor exclaimed.

Meanwhile, back at home, Mabel thought
about how she might convince the mayor.

Night had already fallen when the mayor opened Mabel's email.

"When was the last time you saw thousands of stars?"

The mayor closed her eyes.

Long ago, lying on a striped blanket under the darkest of summer skies, she had tried to count them all.

The mayor opened her eyes.

"Okay," she typed, *"let's try it."*

On the next new moon, people arrived on
the hill with dogs and blankets and snacks.

They saw bright stars and dim stars, Venus and Mars,
white stars, golden stars, and stars of the hottest blue.

"Now, this is what I call stargazing," Grandpa said. "How many up there, Mabel?"

But Mabel was looking around instead. There was quite a crowd! And a little down the way, the mayor sat on a striped blanket, gazing up at the sky.

"I haven't even started to count," Mabel told Grandpa.

A tradition began that night. People gathered every
new moon, bringing telescopes, binoculars, egg salad
sandwiches, and strawberry pie.

Each time, the sky was a little darker as lights-out spread
from street to street. Everyone saw meteor showers
and the Milky Way, planets, constellations, and satellites.

Mabel wondered if she would ever count them all —
those stars just up the street.

There were definitely thousands!